The Cranberries that Didn't Fit In

With bonus Theatre Script

By David Flack

This book is dedicated to my band, David Flack and the Paradigm Shifters.

Bonus Theatre Script begins on page 13.

Designed and Illustrated by Beverly Pearl

Production : H&S Le Temps H&S Times
http://www.tempshstimes.com/

ISBN: 9798745968549

About the Author

David Flack grew up in Western Hill, St. Catharines in the 1950's and 1960's. The City of St. Catharines is well known for its Grape and Wine Festival held in late September. At Brock University David completed courses that included "Drama to 1642" and "Theatre Practice" and then went on to obtain a B.Ed. and Teaching Certificate in English and Dramatic Arts. Being a sort of Renaissance character, though, he also published a book "Statistics Primer" in 1974 after having helped many a student in their Statistics

course. In 1984 he was one of 3 authors of "History Through Drama", a sourcebook for teachers of Dramatic Arts.David spent a number of years as a teaching assistant in the Department of Geography at Brock University being a lab instructor in courses such as Physical Geography, Maps, Remote Sensing, Surveying, Meteorology, and G.I.S. He was also a professor in the Post-Grad G.I.S. program at Niagara College.

After retiring in 2007, he took up the guitar, started writing songs, formed a band called "David Flack & the Paradigm Shifters" and released his debut CD, "Not Your Typical Average" in 2016,followed by an EP, "Cranberries In Song", In 2020 he wrote this play which promotes acceptance of diversity and a concern for saving the planet's future, in this instance, the survival of bees facing the threat of neonicotinoids.

The pink cranberries are symbolic of anyone who suffers from rejection due to simply being "different". The message of the play is that we are all one.

Forward

This story follows the plot line of a play that I wrote in the fall of 2020 and goes by the same title. The play is a musical with parts of songs from "David Flack & the Paradigm Shifters". In 2018 we released an EP titled "Cranberries In Song" featuring three original songs about cranberries. You may listen to these songs at the following site:
www.thenewparadigmshifters.bandcamp.com

You may also want to listen to Madison Galloway's song "Bye-Bye" with reference to the scene in the play and the book concerning the Bee and the Neo-Nics.

Watch for a possible sequel as the Pink Cranberries go on to become a musical sensation but have to deal with the Neo-Nics and the dilemma of female bands making it in the music industry.

 We would be most appreciative to hear feedback from you. What did your children think of this book? My contact e-mail is **dflack@gmail.com**.

Happy reading and may you "Add cranberries to your day".

"When you want to teach children to think,
you begin by treating them seriously when
they are little, giving them responsibilities,
talking to them candidly, providing privacy
and solitude for them, and making them
readers and thinkers of significant thoughts
from the beginning. That's if you want to
teach them to think."

— Bertrand Russell

Some time ago, Crispland, a tiny little village in OntaroLand began an annual cranberry festival which grew more and more respectable.
The people there were proud of their "red and sour" cranberries that grew in a bog near some blueberries.

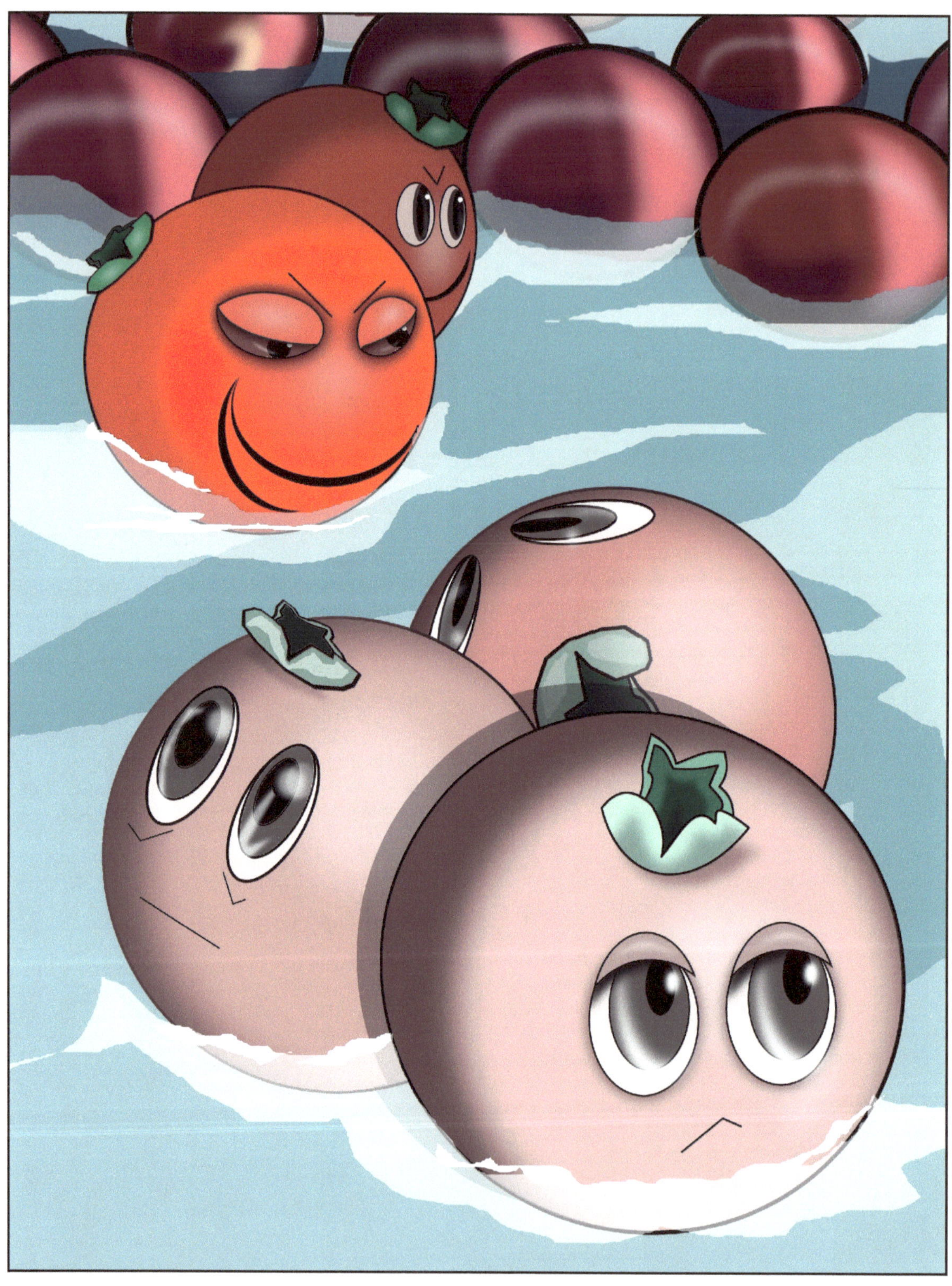

One year, though, some of the berries turned out "sweet and pink". These poor berries were taunted by the others who chanted "People won't care for you, we don't think".

The Cranberry Festival Manager, upon seeing the current year's crop, exclaimed "I'm gobsmacked; these will never do, they are sure to be a flop".

Meanwhile, the "red and sour" berries were preparing for pollination by the Bee.
The Bee was happy to do its work, but then arrived the "Neo-Nics", you see.

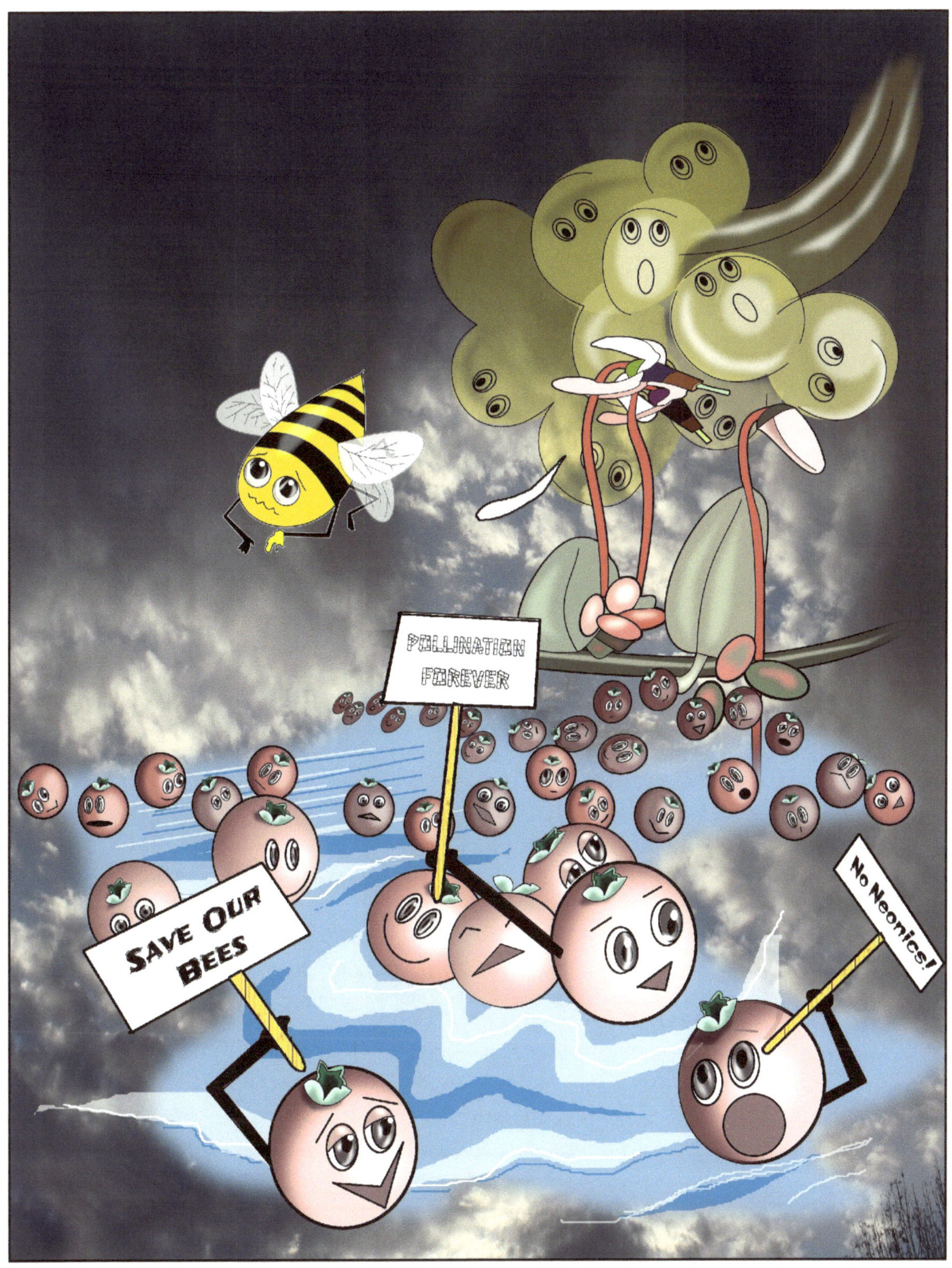

The Neo-Nics believed they were doing the berries a favour with their spray but in the process weakened the Bee in a very bad way. The "red and sour" berries were worried, but a couple of the pink ones had an idea. They got on their cell phones, spread the word, and gathered signatures as of the Neo-Nics all the world heard.

The protest worked, the Neo-Nics were banned, but the Cranberry Festival Manager still would not let the pink berries be a part of the festival as planned.

The "red and sour" berries felt bad for the pink ones who had helped them defeat the Neo-Nics and came up with a plan to get them on a train to GreatLand, which had a festival that welcomed all grapes, purple, blue, red, didn't matter what their politics.

So as one of the many trains that passed through this tiny town slowed down at the bridge, the "red and sour" berries helped get their pink cousins aboard the train and across the ridge.

On arrival in GreatLand, the pink berries met a group of grapes sobbing away. "O what is the matter", asked the pink berries. "O, the situation is dismal, we are nothing but tearful, perhaps the new name will fizzle, it's got us in a real pickle" they proclaimed. The grapes explained to the pink berries that what was once a "Grape and Wine Festival" had become just a "Wine Festival".

So the pink berries tried again using social media for support. "Expose the corruption, give the new name a rejection, reveal the deception", they typed away on their cell phones. The campaign worked, thousands signed, and the name was restored to "Grape and Wine Festival".

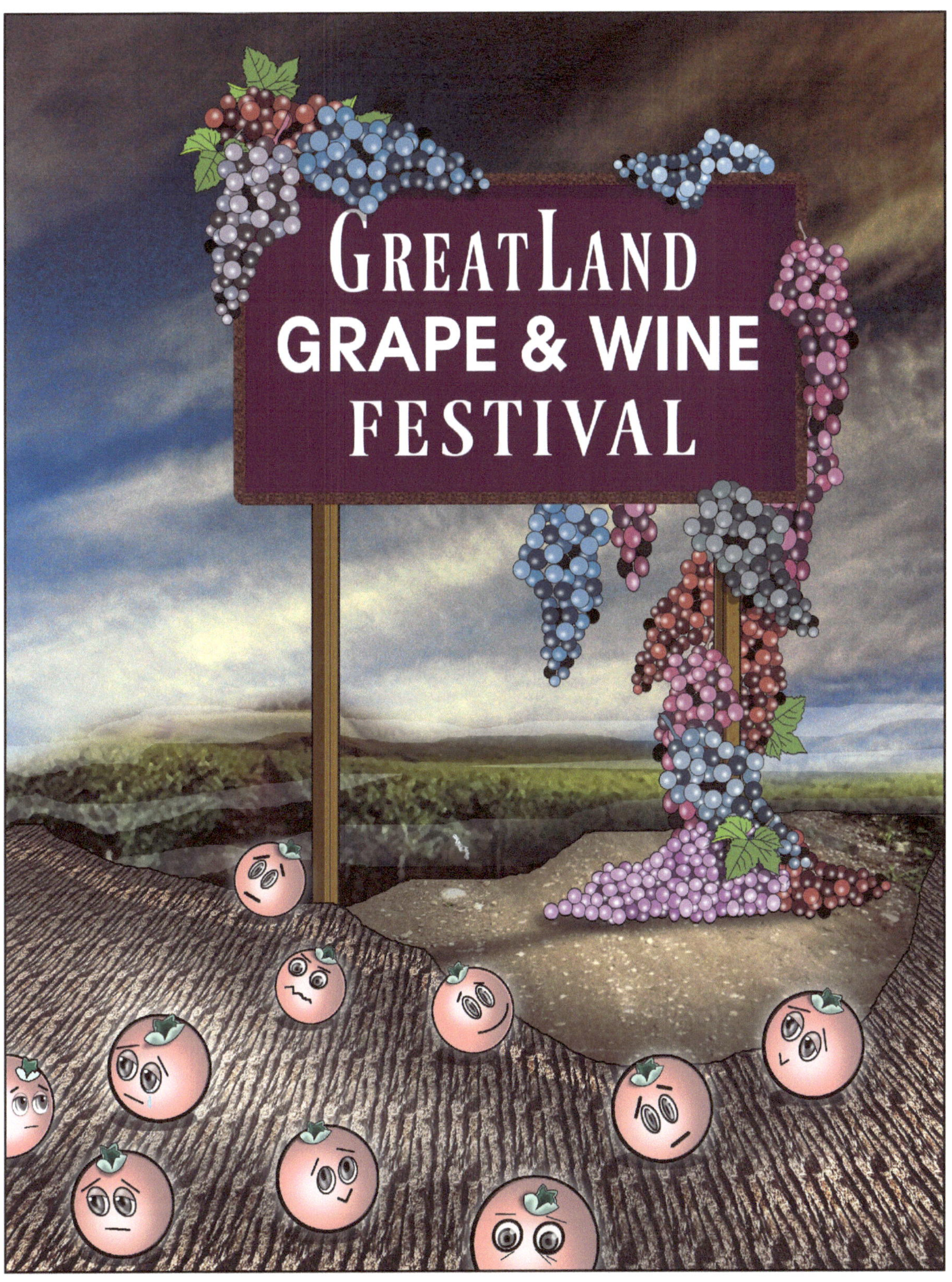

The grapes were very thankful for the help from the berries and welcomed them most heartily. The berries, though, still felt homesick and rather out-of-place in a grape festival so certainly..

All turned out well, though, as a new Crispland Cranberry Festival Manager came down to GreatLand and welcomed the "sweet and pink" berries back to the Cranberry Festival. The new manager told of how new people were now in charge, people who welcomed difference. The manager even invited the grapes to take part in the cranberry festival. "We are all one" they sang together in this new age of tolerance. And so, both festivals grew to be even better as things were now in harmony right down to the letter.

The Cranberries that Didn't Fit In
Theatre Script

By David Flack

Musical Selections by David Flack & Madison Galloway

Forward for the Play

This play is meant to appeal to both children and adults. Children will love the cranberry and grape characters and adults should like some of the themes such as acceptance of diversity and environmental responsibility. Some of the vocabulary will be beyond children's familiarity, in fact may even be beyond that of many adults. However, the rhyming of the "big words" will add to their appeal and should be understandable within the context of the play's action.

The play is somewhat political such as the reference to the 2020 election in U.S.A. but these parts may be deleted should it not be relevant to your audiences.

The music could be played as audio only but ideally one would have a live band on stage performing the songs.

Potential users of this script are welcome to message me **(dflack@gmail.com)** for whatever help I can give towards your production of this play.

Synopsis

While the Cranberries are anticipating the upcoming Cranberry Festival, they notice some which are 'pink and sweet 'rather than 'red and sour'. Āfter some taunting, the Cranberry Festival Manager rejects the oddities. Meanwhile as the cranberries wait to be pollinated, the arrival of the Bee is interrupted by the Neo-Nics. The pink berries help to defeat the Neo-Nics, but are still rejected by the Cranberry Festival Manager.

The red cranberries help their counterparts escape the compost pile by sneaking them aboard a train that takes them to Niagara. On arrival the pink berries meet some grapes that are crying in sorrow. It is discovered that what was once a Grape and Wine Festival had been re-named a Wine Festival. The pink berries come to the rescue again, restoring the original name of a Grape and Wine Festival. All ends well when a Farmer discovers these pink and sweet cranberries to be the perfect ingredient for a new Cranberry Grape Juice. A new Cranberry Festival Manager arrives to invite the Pink Cranberry back to a Cranberry Festival that now celebrates diversity and even extends an invitation to the Grapes to be a part of it as well.

Index

Songs Used in the Play

"O Cranberry"
"Add Cranberries to Your Day"
"An Ode to Cranberries"
"Bye-Bye" (song by Madison Galloway)
"Don't You Dare Step on Their Toes"
"Paradigm Shift"
"Give Love A Chance"

Here are the links to listen to the songs:
www.thenewparadigmshifters.bandcamp.com
www.madisongallowaymusic.bandcamp.com

Here is contact information for David Flack and Madison Galloway:
dflack@gmail.com
madisongallowaymusic@gmail.com

Characters:

Red Cranberry 1
Red Cranberry 2
Red Cranberry 3
Pink Cranberry
The Bee
Neo-Nic1
Neo-Nic2
Cranberry Festival Manager
Grape 1
Grape 2
Grape 3
Grape & Wine Festival Manager
Farmer
The New Cranberry Festival Manager
Musicians (3)

(C) (C) (C) Oh Cranberry of genus (D) Vaccinium macrocarpon

(C) Low creeping shrub in (E) acidic bogs where you grow on (E)

(G) Rich source of polyphenols for the (D) health of us all

(C) And how red cranberry sauce makes (D) plain turkey sparkle

(C) Oh Cranberry so (D) deliciously sour

(C) I do believe you (E) have the power

(G) To add twenty years (D) to my time

(C) Twenty more years (D) feeling fine

(Em) Cranberries so (D) red and sour

(F) How we love (D) you to devour

(Em) In wine, sauce, jam or tarts at (G) any hour

(F) Oh Cranberry do you (G) know your power?

(C) Native people used you for (D) wounds and red dye

(C) And how we love to put you in (E) tarts or pie

(G) You've even given a name to (D) one of my favorite bands

(C) And how we love when you (D) appear in jams

(Em) Cranberries so (D) red and sour

(F) How we love (D) you to devour

(Em) In wine, sauce, jam or tarts at (G) any hour

(F) Oh Cranberry do you (G) know your power?

(during the above song, the cranberries dance around the stage)
(The stage is anything that suggests a cranberry bog)

Cranberry1: Well, only 6 months now until they celebrate us once again at the Cranberry Festival

Cranberry2: Yes, there will be maybe 20 or 30,000 visitors if the weather's right

Cranberry3: Yea, if we don't get that early October snowstorm or freezing rain or bitter cold

Cranberry1: Yea, but thanks to good old global warming, that's a thing of the past now. We're more
likely to get 30 degree heat.

Cranberry3: And those pesky blackflies buzzing all around our heads

Cranberry1: So what do you suppose you might become?

Cranberry2: I'm hoping to be part of a cranberry tart

Cranberry3: And me, cranberry jam

Cranberry1: Well I'd like to dress up someone's Thanksgiving or Christmas turkey

Cranberry2: I hope they have that Silver Elvis again this year

Cranberry3: Yea, he was something else, eh?

Cranberry1: Just think, we've been celebrated now for over 30 years in this small town

Cranberry2: Except for that crazy 2020 where nothing existed, so to speak.

Cranberry1: Well there's been almost half a million visitors over the years. People do love cranberries.

Cranberry3: Or maybe just any excuse to get out and party.
(During the above talk, the Pink Cranberry is staying out of the limelight)

Cranberry1: Say, what's wrong with that cranberry over there?

Cranberry2: Yea, he doesn't look too well

Cranberry3: So pink, what's that all about?

They approach the Pink Cranberry

Cranberry1: What's with the pale demeanour?

Cranberry2: Yea, why so pinky?

Pink Cranberry: G'day Red Cranberries. Well, let me answer in song

Song (Musicians)

(Dm) And it ain't easy to (G) keep us a growin'

(Em) We need lots of water in those (Am) bogs that we float on

(Dm) And water's not something (G) we've done well protecting

(Em) Just like with the bee (Am) it needs defending

Cranberry2: Oh, so you're one of those environmental protesters

Cranberry 1 ***(goes to licking Pink Cranberry):*** Hey, you're not even sour, you're sweet

Red cranberries move away from Pink Cranberry

Cranberry3: Sweetie, sweetie, people won't care for ye

Cranberry2: Sweetie, sweetie, people will avoid ye

Cranberry1: Sweetie, sweetie, people won't buy ye

Pink Cranberry retreats into backstage, feeling dejected.
The Cranberry Festival Organizer arrives, with a look of great expectations

Cranberry Festival Manager: Well, it's going to be a banner year for our festival. Especially after that 2020 disaster of a year. The crop is looking bountiful and everyone in town is just itching to get out and celebrate our treasure, the cranberry. So how are all you berries doing?

Cranberry1, 2 and 3: Feelin 'fine and ready to shine!

Cranberry Festival Manager: Good, that's what I like to hear. Enthusiasm! Love it! Now……wait a minute, what's this? Are my eyes deceiving me? (removes his glasses and wipes them clean) Whoa, what are these? Pink berries? I don't believe this. Well maybe they just need a bit more ripening.

(Takes a taste of Pink Cranberry) Ugh. Sweet. That's not a cranberry. A cranberry is red and sour.

(Turns to the audience delivering this soliloquy)

Egads, these pink berries are good. So deliciously sweet. But wait, if I let them into our festival they will surely steal the spotlight. And I have heard reports about this other town just east of here where the bogs are full of pink berries. Hmmmm…this could likely transfer our festival out of our proud town and into their hands. I cannot afford to sound wishy-washy. I will retain my prejudicial attitude.

(end of soliloquy)

Well these are certainly no good for our festival. What would the people think? I'm just gobsmacked. I can just see all those negative google reviews. Ha, last thing we need. This will never do.

(Takes out cell phone)

Message to staff – Get these pink berries out of the bog. Take them to our compost heap. Maybe they can help nourish our potato patch. Hey, musicians play that Ōde to Cranberries and let's generate some buzz for our upcoming cranberry festival.

Song (Musicians)

(D) (A) (G) (E) (D) O Cranberries, you're so (A) tart and crisp

(G) My lips pucker, my eyes quiver, itš a (E) flavour eclipse

(C) A perfect fruit, a (G) burst of bliss

(A) (D) O Cranberries, always (A) dressed to the nines

(G) With your bright red colour and your (E) glossy shine

(C) You're a ten out of ten (G) in my mind

(D) O Cranberries, thank you for your (A) superior anti-oxidants

(G) Gone are my worries and any (E) infections of consequence

(C) And at 45 calories a cup I can (G) enjoy you with confidence

(D) O Cranberries, you're so (A) tart and crisp

(G) My lips pucker, my eyes quiver, it's a (E) flavour eclipse

(C) A perfect fruit, a (G) burst of bliss

(A) (D) O Cranberries, a (A) perfect Canadian treat

(G) Like hockey, apologies and (E) maple syrup sweet

(C) As a true national icon, I think you're (G) hard to beat

(D) O Cranberries, you're so (A) tart and crisp

(G) My lips pucker, my eyes quiver, it's a (E) flavour eclipse

(C) A perfect fruit, a (G) burst of bliss

(A) (D)(G)(C)(A) (E) (G))D) Fresh, frozen, sauced or (A) dried

(G) Bury me with cranberries (E) if I have died

(C) O Cranberries, call me (G) Thanksgiving for you'll (D) always be my

(C) favourite side

(D) (C) (D)

(The Red Cranberries dance around the stage whilst this song is being played, feeling left out) The Pink Cranberry looks on feeling left out.)

Act 2

The cranberries are sitting on stage looking up and waiting.

Red Cranberry2: Well, here we are waiting for our friend, the Bee. Thank goodness for her help. What would we do without her?

Red Cranberry1: Yes, especially with our market price declining. Maybe we'll survive on tourism, but without our friend, the Bee, we just won't be growing.

(Enter The Bee going from one berry to the other)

The Bee: Oh, I'm so happy pollinating all these berries. It's a mutually beneficial situation.

Red Cranberry1: So happy to see you again, too.

(Enter the Neo-Nics holding sprayers in their hand)

NeoNic1: Rejoice, you cranberries, we have come to help you grow more plump and protect you from disease

NeoNic2: And to help bolster the profits of our makers.

NeoNic1: Shhh...no need to let that be known.

(The NeoNics proceed to go around spraying the Cranberries who look on in bewilderment, not knowing what to think) (As they do this, the musicians play the following song which was written by Madison Galloway)
(The Bee slowly starts to collapse on stage and gasps for breath)

Song (Musicians)

(C) (E) (C) (E) Da de de de da de da

(C) Hello lovely bee

(E) I know we're worried about DDT, like Joni said

(C) But now a new problem on our hands

(E) Thought we were moving forward

But (F) we're just moving (G) back, back, back

(C) It's pretty clear we cannot last

(E) Cause if you go, then so do we

(C) Got to worry 'bout those birds and bees

(E) And all the pretty trees

Oh it's (F) quite concerning (G) me

(C) And if you go, then so do we

(E) Got to worry 'bout those birds and bees

(C) All the butterflies

(E) All that's passing by in the skies

And (F) below on the (G) ground, all around

And pretty soon they'll say 'Bye-Bye'(repeat C E C E)
Fifty thousand dropping dead

(E) But the thought's just passin' above our heads

(C) Like clouds in the sky that roll by

(F) Without a second (G) glance

(C) They got those neo-nic seeds, coated in the palm of their hands

(E) Nothing's ever as it seems

(F) The world's not what it seems (G)\

Instrumental C E C E

(C) Hello lovely bee

(E) I know we're worried 'bout DDT

(F) But please don't fly away (G) I promise we'll mend our ways

(E) Cause if you go then so do we

(C) We got to worry 'bout those birds and bees

(E) And all the pretty trees

(F) Oh it's quite concerning (G) me

(C) And if you go then so do we

(E) We got to worry 'bout those birds and bees

(C) And all the butterflies

(E) All that's passing in the skies

(F) And below on the (G) ground, all around

And pretty soon they say 'Bye-Bye'
(repeat C E C E)

RedCranberry1: Oh no, look what's happened to our friend, the Bee

Neo-Nic1: Nothing to worry about here. It's the price to pay for progress.

RedCranberry1: Balderdash. You've scared the bejeebers out of us. (Neo-Nics depart)

RedCranberry1: This is a disaster. What can we do? The crop will be ruined without the Bee. And that
will be the end of any cranberry festival. Those Neo-Nics have tried to hoodwink us.

RedCranberry2: O, I feel so discombobulated.

Pink Cranberry: So what?

RedCranberry1: He means "confused".

Pink Cranberry: Wait, I have an idea.

(The Cranberries huddle around each other quietly discussing their plan and then typing away on their cellphones)

RedCranberry1: Yes, mount a campaign on social media.

RedCranberry2: Expose the corruption.

RedCranberry3: Expose the deception.

RedCranberry1: Give the bees our protection

RedCranberry2: Give neonicotinoids a rejection

RedCranberry3: Mount an insurrection

RedCranberry1: A what?

RedCranberry3: "A violent uprising against an authority". Well, it rhymes, doesn't it?

RedCranberry2: The Neo-Nics stand guilty of misdirection.

RedCranberry3: Give cranberries an exemption.

RedCranberry1: Draw peoples' attention

Pink Cranberry: Look, It's working. We're getting thousands of signatures. People are venting their protestation.

RedCranberry 1,2,3: Their what?

PinkCranberry: Their emphatic declaration that something is not the case.

(The Neo-Nics return, eyes on their cellphones)

Neo-Nic1: You left-wing trouble-makers. Now you've got us banned. Thank you for your
circumspection.

RedCranberry1,2,3: Our what?

Neo-Nic1: Your unwillingness to take risks.

Neo-Nic2: Yes, thank you for pushing agricultural retroflection, or to put it in words you may
understand, "bending back advances in agriculture".

Pink Cranberry: Sorry, but your intentions were a false pretension.

(The Neo-Nics leave, obviously very upset)

RedCranberry1: Well, thank you Pink Cranberry. You've saved the day. (The Bee starts to recover)

RedCranberry2: We're so sorry for making fun of you earlier on.

RedCranberry3: Yes, what can we do to make it up to you?

Pink Cranberry: Well, we would love to be a part of the cranberry festival.

Red Cranberry 1: Fine, we will ask our festival manager to include you in the program.

(Enter the Cranberry Festival Manager, looking worried)

Cranberry Festival Manager: What's all this hullabaloo about? Has there been a problem?

RedCranberry1: The Neo-Nics were killing off our Bee and, if she goes, we go. Thanks to the help of our Pink Cranberry we were able to overthrow this menace to us and our planet.

Cranberry Festival Manager: Well, all well and good. However, the festival has a reputation to uphold. Cranberries are red and sour, not pink and sweet. Enough of this malarkey. Sorry, but I cannot go along with this imperfection.

Red Cranberry1,2,3: Well fiddle-dee-dee!

Act 3

(The Cranberries are parading around in a circle trying to decide what to do)

Cranberry3: There must be something we can do for our Pink Cranberry

Cranberry2: Yes, unfortunately these rural areas can often be quite narrow-minded , not willing to go along with more progressive views and diversity that seem more popular in the cities

Cranberry1: And wasn't that so apparent when the news channels were showing us all those maps of blue and red back in November 2020?

Cranberry1: Wait, I have an idea. I've heard of a place called Niagara that celebrates its grapes every fall season and they don't care about the color of the grapes. They can be green, they can be purple, they can be red. Why I think they'd even accept yellow.

Pink Cranberry: That sounds like a place where I'd belong.

Cranberry3: But how do we get you there?

Cranberry2: Yes, they've put an end to the bus route that used to come this way. Wasn't that a brilliant move, under a government trying to promote public transportation.

Cranberry1: Ah, but there are still those freight trains that roar through here at least a dozen or more times a day

Cranberry2: Don't we all know that.

Cranberry3: If you can put up with those trains waking you up at all hours of the night, and snow from as early as October to sometimes even in May, and those blackflies and deer flies all summer long, it's a great place to live.

Cranberry2: Well I'd rather endure that then listen to those crazy city folk with their noisy lawnmowers and constant traffic slowdowns and all that construction.

Cranberry1: Okay, here is the plan. We wait for one of those trains to slow down at the bridge, then hold up the pink cranberries and pop them aboard the open cars Pink Cranberry: Sounds good. I'm all in.

(Lights dim.....Sound of a freight train can be heard in the dark)
(Stage scenery changes to suggest a vineyard)

Pink Cranberry: **(exploring the new territory)** Well this looks intriguing, but what is that wailing I hear?

(Grapes 1,2 and 3 wander on stage, crying)

Grape1: Oh, the situation is dismal

Grape2: We are nothing but tearful

Grape3: Yes, ever since they made it official

Grape1: Their change is truly drivel

Grape2: Maybe the new name will fizzle

Grape3: They've really put us in a pickle

Grape1: Made us feel so little

Grape2: Could even call it sinful

Pink Cranberry: G'day Grapes. Why so sad? What situation do you say is bad?

Grape1: Why hello Cranberry. Let me explain. There was once a great festival celebration called a Grape and Wine Festival. There were even floats loaded with real grapes. Nowadays thereš nary a one to be found. But we can understand why that is so. What we cannot understand is the change in the festival's name.

Song (Musicians)

(F/D) Well Niagara's Grape and Wine Festival

(G/D) Became for a while just a Wine Festival

Pink Cranberry: O migosh. That's awful.

(A/D) Thank God it's always been a (Em/D) Cranberry Festival
(D) Poor Grapes

Pink Cranberry: Maybe I can help you, just as I did the Red Cranberries when they were being threatened by the Neo-Nics.

Grapes 1,2,3: Tell us more

(Pink Cranberry and the Grapes huddle together and take out their cellphones)

Grape1: Expose the corruption

Grape2: Expose the deception

Grape3: Give the new name a rejection

Grape1: Draw peoples' attention

Grape2: The new nameš a misdirection

Grape3: Mount an insurrection

Grape 1: Well we don't have to go that far.

Pink Cranberry: Look, we've gained a thousand likes on facebook, two thousand followers on twitter, and even more on Instagram.

Grape1: Yes, and look at all the names on our petition.
(lights dim....Grapes return holding up posters advertising the upcoming Grape and Wine Festival)

Grape and Wine Festival Manager: We apologize for dropping the word "grapes" in the name of our festival. The people have spoken. It will once again be the Grape and Wine Festival.

Grape2: Thank you so much, Pink Cranberry for helping us restore the name of our festival.

(Pink Cranberry and Grapes march off stage)

28

Act 4

(Stage scenery suggests being in the middle of a Grape & Wine Festival celebration)

Grape1: Well, Pink Cranberry, how are you enjoying our festival?

Pink Cranberry: It's a real pleasure, but, being a cranberry, I don't really feel a part of it, as I may have
back there in the Cranberry Festival.

Grape2: Hmmm. I have an idea. Let me introduce you to one of my friends. ***(calls friend on cellphone)***

Farmer ***(now coming on stage):*** Hello, Grape, Happy to see you. How can I help?

Grape2: Our friend here, Pink Cranberry, is feeling a little bit out of place, being a cranberry in a festival about grapes.

Farmer: I may have an idea. Pink Cranberry, would you like to come with me and tour our operation?

Pink Cranberry: Well, thank you. Lead the way.
(Pink Cranberry goes offstage with Farmer, then returns to a stage setting suggestive of a farm)

Farmer: I've been thinking of coming up with a new juice that would combine the flavor of grapes with that of cranberries.

Pink Cranberry: What a swell idea. Let's see how it goes.
(Pink Cranberry and Farmer add grapes and cranberries into a barrel...improvise movement here that would suggest a new juice is being manufactured)
(Grapes show up to join Pink Cranberry and Farmer as they pour out the new juice into glasses and try tasting)

Song (Musicians)

(D) (A) (G) (E) (D) O Cranberry Grape Juice, you're so (A) sweet and crisp

(G) Egads what a taste and camaraderie, it's a (E) flavour eclipse

(C) Two perfect fruits, a (G) burst of bliss

(A) (D) O Cranberry Grape Juice, always (A) dressed to the nines

(G) With your pale pink colour and your (E) glossy shine

(C) You're a ten out of ten (G) in my mind

(D) O Cranberry Grape Juice, you're so (A) sweet and crisp

(G) Egads what a taste and camaraderie, it's a (E) flavour eclipse

(C) Two perfect fruits, a (G) burst of bliss

(A) (D) O Cranberry Grape Juice, a (A) perfect Canadian treat

(G) Like hockey, apologies and (E) maple syrup sweet

(C) As a true national icon, I think you're (G) hard to beat

(D) O Cranberry Grape Juice, you're so (A) sweet and crisp

(G) Egads what a taste and camaraderie, it's a (E) flavour eclipse

(C) Two perfect fruits, a (G) burst of bliss

(C) Two perfect fruits, a (G) burst of bliss

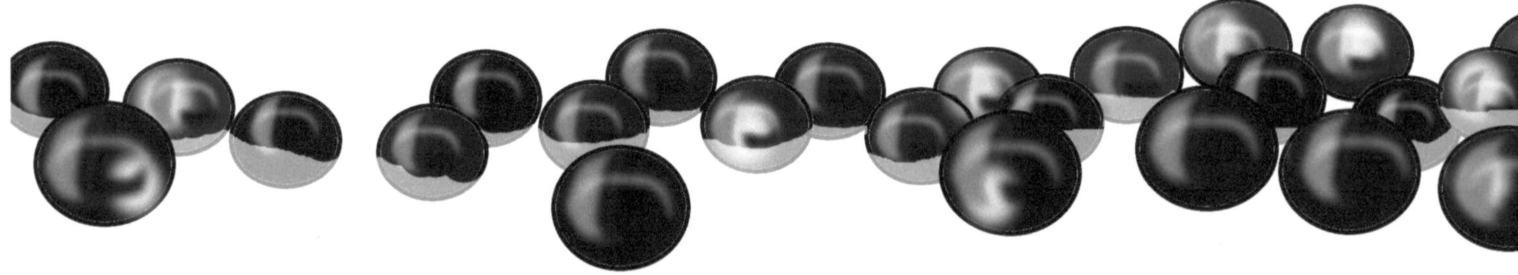

New Cranberry Festival Manager: Greetings all. Let me introduce myself. I am the new Manager of that Cranberry Festival which regrettably rejected you pink berries. Things are different now. It's been a real paradigm shift.

Song (Musicians)

(G) Paradigm (Em) shift…it's around the (G) bend

Paradigm (Am) shift…our world can still (C) mend

(C) So let's not let knuckleheads rule over (D) us

(C) Take their silly shenanigans, throw 'em under the (D) bus

(G) Empathy and kindness…we will (Em) find Ah..ah..ah..ah

(G) Brings to us…peace of (Em) mind Ah..ah..ah..ah

(C) Love surrounds us…no need to (D) run

(C) We're not alone…we all are (D) one

(G) Paradigm (Em) shift …the errors of our past are now un- (G) done

New Cranberry Festival Manager: It was a real kerfuffle back there but eventually there were enough of us who saw the light and were able to change things around. From now on, any berries in that bog that appear different from the norm will be welcomed and form part of a much stronger festival celebration.

Pink Cranberry, please come back and help us make an even better Cranberry Festival.

Pink Cranberry: I'd love to be a part of this, but here I've come to find friendship with these lovely grapes. I think I would miss them sadly.

New Cranberry Festival Manager: Balderdash, you don't need to miss them. They will be welcome as well in our Cranberry Festival. As those musicians just sang "We're not alone….we all are one". It's time to find common ground and heal this increasingly polarized society.

Grape & Wine Festival Manager: And likewise, all you cranberries, both the "pink and sweet" and the "red and sour" are welcome to be a part of our Grape and Wine Festival.

Song (Musicians)

(C) How are you with (G) others different from (D) you?

(C) Why can't you (G) see they matter (D) too?

(G) Can we be (C) nicer if we (D) try?

(C) See the best in (D) all who pass you (G) by

(G) Lend out your (C) heart….(G) Kindness is (C) smart

(G) Treasure (C) diversity…(G) Live life in (D) harmony (C)

Why don't you (G) live life in (D) harmony? (C)

Song (Musicians)

(A) Don't take rejection as (G) personal

(A) Nothing wrong to be (E) controversial

(A) You've nothing much to (G) lose

(A) Give love a chance, you'll get those (E) breakthroughs

32